# I See the Sun in China

# 我看在中国上空的太阳



作者: Dedie King
插图: Judith Inglese

**Written by Dedie King**
**Illustrations by Judith Inglese**

打印在美国

国际标准书号： 978-0-9818720-5-6

翻译严张
书法晗张

如需订购此为您的学校，图书馆，或组织出版的资料，请与我们联系。



Printed in the United States of America

ISBN: 978-0-9818720-5-6
Library of Congress Control Number: 2010928109

Translation by Yan Zhang
Calligraphy by Han Zhang

For information about ordering this publication for your school, library, or organization, please contact us.

Satya House Publications, Inc.
P. O. Box 122
Hardwick, Massachusetts 01037
(413) 477-8743

orders@satyahouse.com
www.satyahouse.com

献给 TULLIO 和 PETER

*For Tullio and Peter*

清晨黎明，一缕阳光照射进我的窗户，爬上了我的脸庞。

我醒了，看到太阳真高兴。

At dawn, sunshine fingers slip through my window and tickle my face.

I wake, happy to see the sun.

我轻声地叫小弟弟起床。

我们一起看爷爷在东方的第一缕晨曦里打太极。

I whisper little brother awake.

Together we watch Grandfather do his Tai Chi in the first east light.

今天，我真激动，因为我要到上海见我的阿姨。

我很快的喝完了粥，这样妈妈就能早点带我去码头赶上早班的渡船。

Today I am excited to go to Shanghai to see my aunt.

I eat my congee quickly so that Mother can take me to the early morning ferry.

当渡船离开普陀山，观音雕像从它那长满岩石的山头朝我俯看。

她那颗慈爱的心指引着渔民们安全回家。

As the ferry leaves the Island of Putuo Shan, Kwan Yin's statue looks down at us from her rocky hill.

Her loving heart guides the fishermen safely home.

晨中时，漂亮的燕阿姨接到了我。她开车带我到了上海。

因为一直仰着头看着高楼大厦，我的头颈开始发酸。

它们竟然比观音还大。

Beautiful Aunt Yen meets the late morning ferry and drives me to Shanghai.

My neck hurts from looking up at the tall buildings.

They are even bigger than Kwan Yin.

At noon we arrive at Auntie's apartment.

I look up to see my friend the sun, but it is hidden in the gray sky.

中午的时候，我们到了阿姨的公寓。

我抬头想看到我的朋友太阳，可它却躲藏在灰色的天空中。

钟点工阿姨做了我最爱的午餐。
我们一起吃了蒸馒头、虾、蔬菜和米饭。

Ayie the cook has made my favorite lunch. Together we eat the steamed buns, shrimp, vegetable, and rice.

平安燈

下午早些时候，阿姨带我去购物。

徐家汇的购物大厦里层层的玻璃和铬闪闪发亮。

我喜欢一边乘着扶梯，一边看着那些穿着时尚的人们。

In the early afternoon Auntie takes me shopping.

The many floors of the Grand Mall at Xu Jia Hui glitter with glass and chrome.

I like to ride the escalators and watch the fancy people.

下午的时候，我们去公园喝茶。

阿姨用手机打着电话，处理她生意上的事。

我看着那些老人打着麻将，一边听着小笼子里的蟋蟀唱着歌。

Mid-afternoon we go to the park to have tea.

Auntie makes business calls on her cell phone while I watch the old men play mah jong and listen to the crickets sing in their little cages.

傍晚，我们穿过小雨到了一家餐厅。

雨水在我的脚下闪闪发光。

In the late afternoon we walk through the rain to a restaurant.

Watery reflections glisten under my feet.

茂昌眼镜

我见到了阿姨的朋友们，我们一边吃饭，一边说说笑笑。

温暖的友谊让我感觉在家中一样。

We meet Auntie's friends and eat and talk and laugh.

The warm friendliness feels like being home in my village.

晚饭后，我们大家在外滩上散步。

当太阳渐渐西去，江面上闪着微微的红光。

大楼里的灯光在黄昏中闪闪发亮，就像一盏盏的小太阳。

After supper we all walk on the Bund.

The river glows red as the sun sets in the west.

In the twilight the lights inside the buildings shine like hundreds of tiny suns.

RIC

晚些时候，我们去做了足疗。

在那里，我们遇见了一起吃晚饭的
建筑师朋友。

我们一起聊天放松。

Later in the evening we go to get a foot
massage.

We see Auntie's friend from dinner,
the architect.

They discuss their business day while we
relax together.

回到公寓，我开始做家庭作业，阿姨在旁边和她美国的商务伙伴打电话。

他的办公室在波士顿，那里还是早晨呢。

Back in the apartment, I study my schoolwork while Auntie calls her American business partner.

It is morning now at his office in Boston.

在我上床睡觉的时候，我回想着今天。我见了这么多东西，遇见这么多不同职业的人。我想到了在乡村里当学校老师的妈妈，和城市里当生意人的阿姨。我想到了爷爷和他的气功，以及阿姨的建筑师朋友。

我将来去做什么呢？

As I go to bed I think about the day. I have seen so many things and so many people with different jobs. I think about my mother the schoolteacher in the village, and my aunt the businesswoman in the city. I think about Grandfather and his energy practices, and Auntie's friend the architect.

What will I be?

见到阿姨的书架上有一尊观音的塑像，我很开心。

我知道在我心里，观音慈悲的心怀会一直指引着我平安的在我的人生道路上走下去。

I am glad to see a small statue of Kwan Yin in Auntie's room.

I know in my heart that Kwan Yin's wisdom will always guide me safely through my nights and days.

## 词汇表

粥：粥是一种稀饭，在中国很受欢迎的早餐之一。它可以不加配料的吃，也可以配搭小块虾，鱼，熟肉，或蔬菜一起吃。

太极：太极是一种古老的，在中国乃至全世界普及的养身练习。据了解，这项被称为内力武术的运动在个人、集体、甚至竞技的环境下都能被练习。随着时间的发展，其动作的精髓已经演变成了像舞蹈一样优雅的姿态。人们为了身体健康和长寿练习太极。直到今天，全国各地的人们依然在清晨聚集在公园里一起练习太极。

观音：观音是佛教人物阿缚卢枳帝湿伐逻（AVOLOKITESVARA）的女性化身。当佛教传入中国的时候，那些富有同情心的教义被称为KARUNA（来自于梵文，可译为慈悲心）。慈悲心是一种能够感知他人的痛苦和磨难，并能够为他们流泪和采取行动的能力。在中国，这种慈悲心和女性的本质联系紧密，因此男性的佛化身成女性形态的观音。观音也被称为慈悲娘娘，或济世者。

外滩：外滩是上海黄浦江沿岸的一条著名的大道。许多著名的建筑都在外滩上。每时每刻都有人在那里漫步，但是晚上是隔江观看浦东灯光和来往游船的最好时间。

普陀山：普陀山岛是上海海岸附近的一个岛屿，也是著名的那座望着海守护水手的观音雕像的家。这里是四大佛教名山普陀山的所在地。同样在这个岛屿上的还有许多致力于修行的寺庙和女修道院。

麻将：麻将是一种在中国流传了上百年的古老战略技术游戏。其过程要求四个人通过拿起和放出小砖块似的棋子来完成。有时候游戏中也带有赌注。直到今天还会在公园里看到一小群人在一起打麻将。

## Glossary

**Congee:** Congee is a rice porridge that is a popular breakfast food in China. It can be eaten plain or with small pieces of shrimp or fish, cooked meat or vegetables.

**Tai Chi:** Tai Chi is an ancient healing exercise practiced throughout China, as well as around the world today. It is known as an internal martial art that can be done alone, in groups, or even in competitions. Over time the essence of the movements evolved into an almost dancelike, graceful form that is practiced for health and longevity. Still today, people all over China gather in parks in the early morning to practice Tai Chi together.

**Kwan Yin:** Kwan Yin is the female embodiment of the Buddha figure Avolokitesvara. When Buddhism came to China, the compassionate teachings were known as karuna. Karuna is the ability to feel other people's pain and suffering, to be able to shed tears for others, and to take action for them. In China, this compassion was more associated with the female essence so the male Buddha was changed to the female form of Kwan Yin. Kwan Yin is also known as the Goddess of Mercy and the protector of all beings.

**Bund:** The Bund is a famous pedestrian boulevard along the Huangpu River in Shanghai. Many architecturally famous buildings are along the Bund. People stroll here at all hours, but the evening is a favorite time to see the lights of Pudong across the river and to watch the boats cruise by.

**Putuo Shan:** Putuo Shan is an island off the coast of Shanghai that is home to the famous statue of Kwan Yin who looks out over the sea and protects sailors. Here too is one of the four sacred Buddhist mountains, Mount Putuo. The island is also the place of many monasteries and nunneries dedicated to Kwan Yin.

**Mah jong:** Mah jong is an ancient game of strategy and skill that has been played for centuries in China. It involves four people, using small tiles to pick up and discard. Sometimes there is betting involved. Still today, one sees small groups of people playing mah jong in the parks.

我看太阳系列丛书用清晰简单的手法描绘了各个国家的一些重要文化元素。在悠久的历史中，中国经历了很多的变化。在最近的50年中，中国拥有越来越多的现代都市，个人的财富也大幅增长，完全实现了从一个低收入的传统社会向一个世界主要经济大国的转变。通过文字和图片，我们试图去抓获那些关于现代中国发展的中心点。

本书的封面用3个主题代表了中国的旧的传统，发展变化和现代社会。如画的帆船代表了久远的历史和旧的生活方式还是存在在当今的生活中。渡轮表现了从旧到现代的转变。上海的建筑则显示了现代化的巨大推力继续将中国推向未来。故事中的元素描绘了今日中国在这三方面的一个融合。

中国是一个国土面积广大，多民族的国家。其中汉族占大部分。15亿人口中，如藏，维吾尔，彝，瑶，蒙古和纳西族等55个少数民族的人口只占8%。由于篇幅所限，本书只能涉及到一个中国的一个方面。本书提到的小女孩和她的家人都是汉族，而上海这个城市则体现了在中国的年轻人从农村移民到城市，从旧到新的转变，以及他们与世界其它部分的联系。

Each book in the ***I See the Sun*** series tries to portray a feeling of the essential cultural elements of a country in a clear and simple way. China has undergone many changes throughout its long history. The last fifty years has seen it transform from a lower income traditional society to a major economic force in the world, with modern cities and increased individual wealth. We try to capture this central idea of movement in today's China through words and pictures.

The cover of the China book symbolizes the three themes of traditional old, movement and change, and the modern society. The picturesque sailing junk represents the old history and lifestyles still present in China today. The ferry shows the movement from the old to the modern, and the buildings of Shanghai show the vast modernization that continues to thrust China into the future. Elements in the story depict the converging of these three aspects of China today.

China is a very large and very diverse country, both in landscape and in peoples. The majority group is Han Chinese. About 8% of the 1.5 billion people belong to a minority group. Tibetan, Uyghur, Yi, Yao, Mongol, and Naxi are a few of the 55 ethnic groups listed by the People's Republic of China. This small book necessarily had to focus on only one part of China. The little girl and her family are Han and the story is about Shanghai because this city epitomizes the movement of young people from the country to the city, the progress of old to new, and the connections to other parts of the world.

平安燈

*To my daughter, Kathrine.*
—SW



Spear Point Photo page 12, Hohokam Human Effigy Jars Photo page 35, and Mimbres Pottery Photo page 45 © Arizona State Museum, University of Arizona, Helga Teiwes, Photographer

The author and publisher would like to thank the staff of the Heard Museum for their patient and gracious assistance in checking this manuscript for accuracy.

Cover and book design by Cathleen O'Brien
Printed in Singapore.
ISBN 0-8118-0012-1

Warren, Scott
Cities in the sand: the ancient civilizations of the Southwest/written and photographed by Scott Warren.
p. cm
Includes index
Summary: Dicusses some of the things archaeologists have learned about three major groups of Indians that lived in the American Southwest: the Anasazi, the Hohokam, and the Mogollon.
ISBN 0-8118-0012-1 (hard) $10.95
1. Indians of North America—Southwest, New—Antiquities—Juvenile literature. 2. Pueblo Indians—Antiquities—Juvenile literature. 3. Hohokam culture—Juvenile literature. 4. Mogollon culture—Juvenile literature. 5. Southwest, New—Antiquities—Juvenile literature. [1. Indians of North America—Southwest, New—Antiquities. 2. Pueblo Indians—Antiquities. 3. Hohokam culture. 4. Mogollon culture. 5. Southwest, New—Antiquities. 6. Archaeology,] Title.
E78.S8W37 1992 91-38818
979' .01—dc20 CIP AC

Distributed in Canada by Raincoast Books,
112 East Third Avenue, Vancouver, B.C. V5T 1C8

Chronicle Books
275 Fifth Street
San Francisco, California 94103
10 9 8 7 6 5 4 3 2

Front Cover Photo: Small cliff dwelling under protective overhang, Utah.
Title Page Photo: Fremont culture petroglyphs at Dinosaur National Monument, Utah.
Endpaper handprints taken from a slickrock wall in Southern Utah.

Still others separated from their own cultural groups to form new groups. Because these changes happened slowly and because they happened to different groups at different times, it is impossible to say when a civilization began and when it ended. Really, there are no beginnings or ends, only continuations. As scientists have studied prehistoric civilizations, they have named these different stages of adaptation. But while archaeologists have categorized these ancient civilizations, it is important to remember that archaeology is not an exact science. Prehistoric Southwesterners cannot truly be categorized. Every civilization—modern or ancient—is made up of unique and individual humans.

As you read this book or as you visit the ruins that are described in it, try to imagine what the individuals of each group were like. What did they wear? Like us, each of these people had his or her own style. Archaeologists often find jewelry, feathers and other ornaments which ancient people used to decorate themselves. What did they do every day? Try to imagine what it would be like to make a basket or a clay pot, or to play music on a flute made from a reed or an animal bone. Think about what might have made these people laugh, what might have made them cry, what kind of beliefs they may have had, what kind of games they may have played.

Like you, they had families. Like you, they had friends. Like you, they had chores and celebrations. Archaeology will probably never be able to tell us these details of prehistoric life, but if you look carefully, ask questions and use your imagination, you might come up with some ideas of your own.

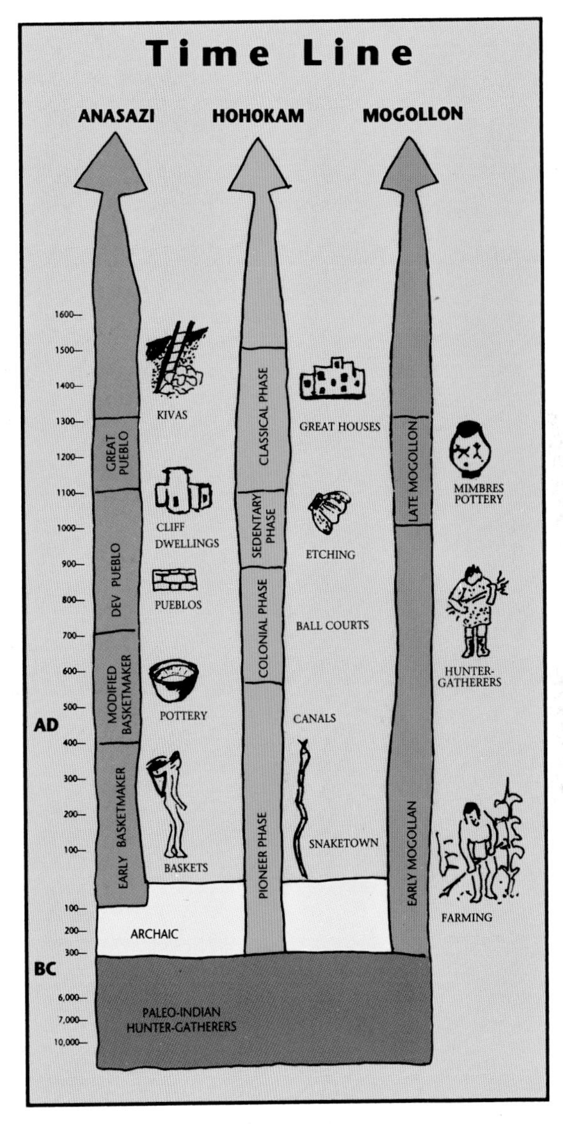


*This time line shows the different stages of the Anasazi, Hohokam and Mogollon groups.*

# CLUES TO THE PAST

The vast number of prehistoric sites found in the Southwest has given archaeologists a tremendous opportunity to study the past. Excavation (or dig) sites can be chosen several different ways. In some cases an area is excavated because the government wants to build roads or other projects. Before this can happen, the area must be surveyed to determine if there are any sections that might contain ancient artifacts. Other sites are chosen by archaeologists after historical research and careful studies of past excavations. Once a site is chosen, archaeologists carefully remove the soil a little bit at a time. Each scoop of dirt is screened for even the tiniest pieces of wood, bone or other remains. In order to analyze the artifact later, it is important to know exactly where each artifact came from. This is why archaeologists take careful notes about everything they find. Often they will make drawings and take photographs of the artifacts and sites as well. Because it is such a slow and careful process, the digging of a single site may take several months, or even years.

*Pottery shards found in southern Utah. By looking at how pots were made, how they were painted and where the clay came from archaeologists can learn a lot about the groups that made them.*

When excavating a site archaeologists sometimes find pottery. Prehistoric South-westerners made a lot of pottery and each group had distinctive techniques for making pots and bowls. By recognizing these different styles, archaeologists can determine not only which group made the pottery but also when it was

*Archaeologists dig an Anasazi ruin at Crow Canyon in Colorado.*

BACARDI

created. By analyzing the clay that was used to create the pottery, archaeologists can even tell if the pot was made locally or if it was imported from somewhere else. This tells us a lot about the trading practices of early times.

When it came to decorating pots, bowls, ladles, jars and other kinds of pottery, different cultural groups also used different colors and patterns. When referring to these different color combinations, archaeologists might say black-on-white, meaning a black design painted on a white slip (or background); or red-on-buff for red designs painted on a buff-colored background. The colors of the pots reflect what was in the environment. Gray pots came from impure clay, while white pots came from very pure clay. Red and black paints came from different kinds of iron deposits found in the soil. Designs etched onto pottery also reflected the artisan's surroundings. For example, people who lived near water often carved images of birds and fish on their pottery because that is what they saw around them.

Other artifacts have their own stories to tell. Shells and tropical bird feathers from Mesoamerica, or Mexico, show that there was probably trade between different areas. Carved turquoise beads, pendants, and earrings suggest that jewelry was important to prehistoric people. Animal bones found in camps reveal what people ate, and spear points and arrowheads offer clues about how they hunted.

Some remains, however, are not so easily understood. Upon countless canyon walls and rock faces throughout the Southwest, prehistoric artists have left behind a vast array of images. Some have been etched or carved into the stone. These are called petroglyphs. Other images, called pictographs, were painted. Included in these panels are images of animals, geometric designs, human figures and supernatural beings. Although fascinating, the actual meanings of prehistoric rock art has puzzled archaeologists for years.

***Prehistoric artisans, like artists today, expressed themselves through paintings, etchings, and carvings. Images etched or carved into stone are called petroglyphs, and images painted on rocks and walls are called pictographs.***

*This petroglyph is called Newspaper Rock and is found at Newspaper Rock State Park, Utah.*

# How old is it?

When looking at a prehistoric ruin or artifact, the question that most often comes to mind is "just how old is it?" To find out, archaeologists have devised a number of dating techniques.

One of the earliest methods of determining the date of an artifact is called stratification. Stratification is the natural layering of material, including artifacts, in the earth. The lower the layer in which an artifact is found, the older the artifact is. Because of stratification, archaeologists are interested in the trash pits and middens (mounds) that early Southwesterners left behind.

*Yellow tags indicate stratified layers in a dig in southeastern Utah.*

Although stratification will always be an important tool for determining the age of a site or artifact, other techniques have been developed that are much more accurate. One of the most important is called dendrochronology, and can determine the age of wooden artifacts. This process was discovered by an astronomer named A.E. Douglass in 1929, and archaeologists were quick to adapt this new science to the study of prehistoric people. For instance, by looking at the rings of the roof beams of a structure they can determine what year the trees that were used to make the beams were cut down and, therefore, they can guess when the dwelling was built. In order to be accurate, archaeologists need to look at a large number of beams. A single beam might turn out to be wood that was used for repairs, in which case it would not help to determine when the dwelling was built.

*This log shows the tree rings used in the dendrochronolgy dating technique, Chaco Culture National Historic Park, New Mexico.*

***In 1929, an astronomer named A.E Douglass realized that the amount of rain that falls each year is reflected in the growth rings of certain weather-sensitive trees, like pine and fir. A year of little rain will result in a thin, dark growth ring, while wetter years produce wider, lighter growth rings. Using this information, Douglass was able to make a master time line showing seasonal changes going back thousands of years.***

Of course, dendrochronology only works when studying artifacts made from wood. Since many early Southwesterners lived in caves or small brush shelters, determining dates for them is more complicated. Radiocarbon dating is perhaps the best method of telling the age of both wooden and non-wooden artifacts. Radiocarbon dating can work on anything that once lived, including bones, shell, wood, flesh and plant remains. Archaeologists measure a certain kind of carbon, called radiocarbon, in materials they find in order to determine how old they are. The longer the object has been dead, the less radiocarbon it has left in it. This dating technique only works on objects that have lived within the past 50,000 years.

Archaeologists are still developing new and more effective ways of determining the age of artifacts that may someday shed more light on the people that first lived in the Southwest. But, like any science, as more answers are found, new questions will arise.

# SETTING THE STAGE

While no one knows for certain, it is generally believed that the first people who moved into the Southwest migrated into North America over a strip of land between Alaska and Siberia. This happened many, many years ago (perhaps as long as 20,000-40,000 years ago) during the Ice Age. When the Ice Age ended, large glaciers melted, covering up the land bridge and creating the body of water we call the Bering Strait.

*Archaic pictograph in Canyonlands National Park, Utah.*

Although the exact date of these first crossings is unknown, it is thought that they occurred when hunters followed herds of game. We call these early hunter-gatherers Paleo-Indians. As they traveled into the region now known as the southwestern United States, these first Americans found a great abundance of wild animals, many of which are extinct today: woolly mammoths, mastodons, prehistoric horses and camels, gigantic bison and slow-moving ground sloths.

Because Paleo-Indians were always on the move, it has been difficult to study their culture. Paleo-Indian sites are hard to find, and when they are found, they are usually little more than a hunting camp. Most of what we know about Paleo-Indians is based on the hunting tools they made. In fact, archaeologists identify different

*Southern Utah canyon country, homeland of the Anasazi.*

*Because Paleo-Indians were constantly moving, most of what we know about them is based on the tools they made. These people were skillful hunters, for they managed to kill and butcher gigantic animals with only small, handmade, stone tools.*

*Clovis spear points, Naco and Lehner sites.*

Paleo-Indian groups by their distinctive spear points.

Although earlier groups of Paleo-Indians may have inhabited the Southwest, the oldest confirmed finds date back 11,000 years. During this time, the region received more rainfall than it does today and lush grasslands were common. The first of these early residents of the Southwest have been named Clovis after an important site discovered near Clovis, New Mexico.

The Clovis people made a variety of tools, including stone knives, scrapers, spear-throwing sticks, called atlatls, and distinctive leaf-shaped Clovis points. The abundance of mammoth bones found at Clovis sites tells us that these animals were a favorite food of these early hunters. The fact that they could successfully hunt such a huge beast tells us that they were skillful hunters and toolmakers.

Another Paleo-Indian group that was highly skilled at hunting is the Folsom, named after a site found near Folsom, New Mexico. Prior to the discovery of this site in 1926, it was thought that

humans had lived in the New World for only 5,000 years. Because of this dig, however, it became clear that the Folsom had lived in the area much earlier—perhaps as long ago as 9000 B.C..

Other Paleo-Indian groups also lived in the Southwest, but eventually, a change in the climate brought the Paleo-Indian way of life to an end. Many large prehistoric animals became extinct and the grasslands disappeared. An arid desert climate, similar to the one found in the Southwest today, spread across the region. By 5500 B.C., a new era of human habitation known as the Archaic tradition had begun.

Although Archaic people still hunted, they concentrated on smaller game, such as deer, bighorn sheep, rabbits, and birds. More importantly, they spent a lot more time foraging for wild plants. Because of this, they inhabited many more areas of the Southwest than the Paleo-Indians had. They also made different tools. Since they hunted smaller animals, the spear points of the Archaic groups

**QUESTION**

**Can you imagine trying to protect yourself from a huge, charging animal, with only sticks and stones to help you? It sounds almost impossible, but ancient people were very good at using just sticks and stones to defend themselves and to hunt large animals. Can you think of ways you might make hunting tools?**

*A variety of artifacts, including old corn cobs, found at a cliff dwelling in Utah.*

*Metates, corn cobs, and other artifacts in Grand Gulch, Utah.*

**QUESTION**

**Where does the water you drink and the food you eat come from? What do you think archaeologists will learn about you from the food you leave behind?**

were smaller than those of the Paleo-Indian hunters had been. Snares and nets made out of plant fiber were also used. And, in addition to making tools for butchering meat, they created tools for chopping, milling, and grinding seeds, nuts, roots, and wild plants. Included in these tools were the first *metates* and *manos*, or grinding basins and stones.

Rather than traveling great distances in search of game, the Archaic people made seasonal migrations that led them to the best sources of food and water. This often meant returning to the same areas at certain times of the year to harvest crops of wild berries, seeds, or nuts. Finding shelter in caves, they sometimes stayed in an area long enough to construct low stone walls for sleeping circles and pits for storing food. At the same time, their population began to grow and new ideas were beginning to filter in from Mesoamerica. As these ideas took root, life in the Southwest changed dramatically.

Of these new ideas, the most important was the concept of growing food. By 5000 B.C., or nearly 7,000 years ago,

Mesoamerican cultures had domesticated corn from a wild grass known as *teosinte*. Although the exact date is still unknown, the earliest evidence of corn in the Southwest dates as far back as 4,000 years. Squash was also introduced early on, and beans followed many years later.

At first, Archaic people had little use for agriculture. They probably sowed a few seeds in places they knew they would return to later in the year, but because their traditional life of hunting and gathering provided them with enough food, the idea of tending crops full-time did not interest them. Why, then, did the prehistoric people of the Southwest eventually become farmers?

Although archaeologists once assumed that the Archaic people became farmers out of choice, new theories suggest that there were very specific reasons for this change. During the later centuries of the Archaic period, the Southwest experienced a dramatic growth in population. This expansion may have depleted natural sources of food and in order to have enough food for everyone, the Archaic people may have planted more crops. Growing and storing their own food also helped them survive times of drought. For whatever reasons, while they still hunted game and gathered wild plants, the Archaic people began to rely more and more on the crops they grew themselves. In order to tend their fields, permanent villages were established and a settled lifestyle began. Other influences, such as pottery, continued to flow in from Mesoamerica and before long, the spectacular civilizations of the prehistoric Southwest began to take shape.

While many other lesser known groups also thrived in this region, the Anasazi (an-uh-saw-zee), the Hohokam (ho-ho-kom), and Mogollon (mo-gee-on) are the three most known people of the prehistoric Southwest. Each of these groups is discussed in the following pages.

***Agriculture became important in the Archaic lifestyle because it helped people survive drought and other harsh environmental conditions, it provided food for a growing population, and it allowed for a settled lifestyle. The earliest evidence of corn in the Southwest dates as far back as 4,000 years. Squash was introduced early on, and beans followed later.***

# THE ANASAZI

The best known prehistoric people of the Southwest are the Anasazi. The name Anasazi is a Navajo word that means "ancient ones" or, more accurately, "enemy ancestors." We do not know what the Anasazi called themselves.

*Betakin Cliff Dwelling at Navajo National Monument, Arizona.*

Although archaeologists disagree on the exact date, the Anasazi probably first appeared as a distinct people by 100 B.C..The Anasazi were different from Archaic people because they relied more completely on food they grew themselves and they built permanent homes. The very largest of their dwellings contained hundreds of rooms and housed many people.

The first Anasazi period is called the Early Basketmaker phase and lasted until 400 A.D. Although the Anasazi did not make pottery at this time, they did make fine baskets. Some were so tightly woven that they could hold water. These baskets were good for storing food, but they could not be set directly on a fire. The early Anasazi cooked by placing hot rocks into baskets filled with water.

*Cliff Palace at Mesa Verde National Park, Colorado.*

*The Basketmakers are best known for their beautiful, woven baskets, but they also wove bags, sandals, and aprons from fiber, and made blankets from rabbit fur and deer skin. They crafted cradle boards to hold their infants on their backs as well.*

Besides making beautiful baskets, the Basketmakers also wove sandals out of yucca fiber and they made cradle boards for carrying infants on their backs. They grew corn and squash. They used *metates* and *manos* to grind corn into meal. They built food storage bins lined with slabs of stone. Their homes were simple, round structures made of sticks and mud and built in shallow caves along canyon walls and cliff faces. These caves protected the Anasazi from the weather. They also helped preserve Basketmaker remains for many centuries.

The next Anasazi period began around 400 A.D. and is called the Modified Basketmaker phase. In order to be near their crops, the Anasazi were now building their villages in open areas near farmland rather than living in caves. During this time, the Anasazi began building more permanent homes called pit houses because they were built partially underground. These "pit houses" included a main living area and a smaller side chamber. A central fire pit, used for both cooking and heat, was located in the larger room and benches sometimes lined the walls. Entry into the structure was usually by ladder through a hole in the roof.

*This Basketmaker site includes food storage cists in a well protected cave, southeast Utah.*

Another important addition that came about during the Modified Basketmaker period was pottery. Although the Anasazi still made baskets, they started making clay pots as well. Before

*Anasazi pots on display at Keet Seel in the Navajo National Monument, Arizona.*

**QUESTION**

**What do we use clay for today? Do you think the Anasazi used pottery for the same purposes?**

this time, clay was sometimes used to line baskets, but true pottery had not yet been used by the Anasazi. Their first ceramic pieces were mostly gray with no painted designs. Like agriculture, it is thought that the craft of pottery came to the Southwest from Mesoamerica and it may have been passed on to the Anasazi by the Mogollon people that lived to the south.

Since the Anasazi now had pots, they could cook directly on a fire. This meant they could boil beans and so beans became a more regular crop. During the Modified Basketmaker period, the Anasazi

began using the bow and arrow, a weapon that made hunting easier. Turquoise jewelry also became popular.

In 700 A.D., the Anasazi entered what archaeologists call their Developmental Pueblo phase. The word pueblo is Spanish for "city," and these pueblos show us that the Anasazi were beginning to live in much larger groups. During this period, Anasazi homes were generally rectangular and built aboveground. Initially made of sticks packed with mud (called waddle-and-daub construction), these buildings were eventually made of masonry, or stone blocks and mud mortar. Because pit houses were warmer in the winter, archaeologists still wonder why this change occurred. The switch may have resulted because a growth in population

## QUESTION

**What are some of the tools and machines used in building houses today? How do you think the Anasazi carried all the rocks and wood needed to build their homes? How did they build without using hammers, nails or saws?**

*Detail of Anasazi masonry at Pueblo Bonito, Chaco Culture National Historic Park, New Mexico.*

***Kivas are underground social and religious centers. Modern descendants of the Anasazi still use kivas, and they remain important centers of religious activity.***

*Kiva at Pecos National Monument, New Mexico.*

required better food storage facilities. Around this time, the Anasazi also started building underground structures called kivas. Usually round, kivas were underground rooms where ceremonies were held. Smaller kivas were about 30 feet across. These probably served small groups of people such as clans, or family groups. Others measured over 60 feet across. It is believed that these larger kivas may have served an entire community or region. Among the modern day descendants of the Anasazi—the Hopi, Zuni and Pueblo Indians—kivas are important centers of religious activity. Because kivas are still used by the descendants of the Anasazi, we can guess how they functioned, but the details of the prehistoric ceremonies remain a mystery.

The Developmental Pueblo phase brought about changes in Anasazi pottery as well. Pots now had a textured finish which meant that they had more outer surface area so heat could be transferred more efficiently when cooking. These corrugated, or ribbed, pots were always plain gray, but other ceramic pieces were painted with beautiful designs.

During the Developmental Pueblo phase, the Anasazi stretched across much of the northern half of the Southwest. The climate was good for farming and the Anasazi learned new ways of using rainwater. They built reservoirs, dams, and terraces that helped capture run-off water that they could use to irrigate their crops. However, the most dramatic changes during this period took place in what is now northwestern New Mexico. Here, in the broad and arid Chaco Canyon, a group of Anasazi built twelve large pueblos. The largest, Pueblo Bonito, covered three acres and housed an estimated 1000 people. It took 150 years to complete.

With Chaco Canyon as a hub, the Anasazi created a system of roads that was some 400 miles long. These roads were 30 feet wide and they radiated out in all directions connecting the pueblo

*Pueblo is the Spanish word for "city". The largest Anasazi pueblo is called Pueblo Bonito, and it spans three acres in Chaco Culture National Historic Park in New Mexico. It housed an estimated 1000 people and took 150 years to build.*

*Above: Pueblo Bonito at Chaco Culture National Historic Park, New Mexico.*

*Next Page: Cliff Palace at Mesa Verde, Colorado.*

with smaller villages. Because the Anasazi did not have wheeled carts or beasts of burden, such as mules or oxen, the purpose of these roads is still a mystery. It is known that in order to build the pueblos nearly 200,000 logs had to be hauled by hand from great distances. Certainly a roadway would have helped with such a task. But it is also believed that these roads may have symbolically linked all the Anasazi communities together.

Beginning around 1100 A.D , the Anasazi entered what is known as the Great Pueblo phase. This period is best known for its architecture. Among the new kinds of buildings the Anasazi constructed were the cliff dwellings that we now see in many national parks and monuments. Like today's apartment buildings, these terraced structures could reach nearly five stories and shelter hundreds of people. The largest of these is Cliff Palace at Mesa Verde National Park in southwest Colorado. It had a total of 217 rooms and 23 kivas.

The construction of cliff dwellings required considerable building skills but exactly why they were built is still unclear. Early theories have suggested that they were built for protection. Some historians believe that during this phase, the Anasazi were being raided by nomadic tribes. Because many cliff dwellings are difficult to climb, they would have provided excellent defense against invasion. In

***The first national park in the United States to be dedicated to the works of man was Mesa Verde National Park in southwest Colorado. The park was founded in 1906 with the main purpose of preserving the remains of the Anasazi.***

order to climb to the top stories, the Anasazi often used ladders. If they were attacked, they could simply lift up the ladders, leaving their enemies with no way to get inside. But archaeologists now believe there may have been other reasons the cliff dwellings were built as well. One of these was the need for more farming land. By moving to the cliffs, the Anasazi freed up valuable flat ground that could be used for growing food. Another reason may have been that these alcoves were warmer in the winter. Cliff dwellings usually face the south so that they can catch more winter sun. The rock itself works like a solar panel, keeping the rooms of the cliff dwelling warm.

But cliff dwellings were not the only structures built during the Great Pueblo phase. During this time, large pueblos and tower-like structures were built on the mesa tops and canyon floors. Several of these towers can be found at Hovenweep National Monument. Built upon the rims of shallow canyons, these towers rise above the stark sagebrush-covered

*Cliff dwelling at Bandelier National Monument, New Mexico.*

*Hovenweep Tower at Hovenweep National Monument, Utah.*

desert. What purpose they may have served is not clear, although one structure, Hovenweep Castle, does include holes in the wall that line up with the sun during the summer solstice.

The Great Pueblo Anasazi were also good traders. Turquoise was exchanged with Mesoamerican cultures for tropical birds, copper bells and shells. Pottery and food were also regularly traded. Such widespread trade helped to spread the Anasazi's ideas even further throughout the region and introduced new ideas from Mesoamerica. Religion was also important during the Great Pueblo period. During this time, the Anasazi built many kivas, including the great kiva at Aztec National Monument.

During the Great Pueblo period the Anasazi began to group their communities together in even larger cities. The largest of these cities

*LEFT: Hovenweep Tower at Hovenweep National Monument, Utah.*

*BELOW: Interior of Great Kiva at Aztec National Monument, New Mexico.*

**QUESTION**

**What are some of the natural resources of your community? Where would you go if suddenly your community lost its natural resources like water and open land?**

often became the hub for entire regions and their influence in the arts, architecture and social life was felt in the nearby villages. Eventually, however, the Anasazi started to abandon their homes. Exactly why they left is not known, but there are several theories.

According to tree ring studies, a drought that lasted 100 years occurred at the end of this period. It is possible that this may have been enough to force the Anasazi away, but droughts were nothing new to these desert people and so this may not be the only reason that they left. Another theory suggests that they may have been driven away by warring nomadic tribes, but concrete evidence of this has not been found. A more recent theory suggests that because of overpopulation, the trees were all cut down to make homes and as a result the topsoil became depleted. Such an environmental disaster would have left them with no fertile ground to farm and no wood for fires, forcing the Anasazi to leave in search of new lands. Besides explaining why the Anasazi may have disappeared, this offers our own civilization a valuable lesson about taking care of natural resources.

Many archaeologists believe that it was probably a combination of all of these reasons that led the Anasazi to abandon their homeland. Within a few years, the Anasazi drifted to the south and southeast where they joined other pueblo dwellers and established new towns and villages. The Hopi Nation in Arizona, Zuni Land in western New Mexico, and the Rio Grande Valley of northern and central New Mexico are some of the places where the Anasazi relocated. Some of these communities have since been abandoned and are now included in several national monuments. Others, such as the Hopi and Zuni villages, and several of the Rio Grande Pueblos, are still occupied by modern day descendants of the Anasazi.

*A Pueblo Indian gathering at Taos Pueblo in northern New Mexico.*

# THE HOHOKAM

A Pima Indian word for "those who have gone," the name Hohokam sheds some light on what became of these ancient people. Where the Hohokam came from, though, is still unclear. One theory suggests that the Hohokam were a branch of Archaic people who were living in the area prior to the Hohokam. Another hypothesis is that they descended from a group of Mesoamericans who had moved into the area because of its flowing rivers. Whatever their origin, Hohokam farmers had established permanent villages along the Salt and Gila Rivers as early as 300 B.C..

*The Agave, or Century plant, was an important food for prehistoric people.*

The Hohokam were different in many ways from other prehistoric people of the Southwest. To make their crops grow in this land of little rain, they used irrigation. While other groups diverted run-off water, the Hohokam actually diverted running rivers, which provided them with continuous irrigation for their crops. Throughout their entire territory, the Hohokam built over 600 miles of canals. The Hohokam were so skilled at constructing them that many modern canals in the area follow their ancient waterways. Canal building, like many other traditions of the Hohokam, such as the practice of

*Saguaro cacti were important plant species in the deserts where the Hohokam lived.*

*In addition to being great canal builders, the Hohokam people were talented craftmakers. They fashioned pendants, bracelets and rings from beads and shells. They shaped bowls from hard stone and decorated them with carved images and they made figurines of clay.*

cremating their dead instead of burying them, was learned from their Mesoamerican neighbors to the south. The Hohokam were tied more closely to Mesoamerica than to any of the other southwestern civilizations.

This first phase of the Hohokam culture is called the Pioneer phase and it lasted until 550 A.D.. One of the earliest Hohokam villages is called Snaketown. The Pima Indians named the site for the large number of snakes they found there during the nineteenth century. Snaketown was inhabited for more than 1,000 years and the site has provided much of the information we now know about the Hohokam. Over the centuries, the Hohokam built some 5,000 dwellings across this large town site. The site has been excavated twice, but archaeologists have only begun to uncover its artifacts. The site is now covered to preserve it for future study. A visit to Snaketown today would reveal little more than several low mounds in the desert.

Because it is located in the open, the Snaketown site suggests that the early Hohokam did not need protection against invaders. It also shows that these early people had a great knowledge of their desert environment. Built over a shallow source of groundwater, the Hohokam only had to dig ten-foot wells to find good sources of drinking water. There was plenty of farmable land nearby and, most importantly, the Gila River provided water for crops.

Like Snaketown, most Pioneer Hohokam villages were built along river ways. Built of brush and mud, their houses were usually large and square shaped. Because winters were mild, they did not need the more heat efficient housing, such as pit houses and cliff dwellings, that the Anasazi built.

The Pioneer Hohokam grew crops of corn, squash, beans, and cotton. At first, their pottery was unpainted, although painted designs were eventually added. The Pioneer Hohokam also shaped

**Question**

Look around you. What do you see in your neighborhood that archaeologists might uncover someday in the future? What do you think these objects would tell them about you and your family?

*Hohokoam human effigy jars, from Snaketown.*

clay into small human figurines. They carved bowls and palettes (surfaces upon which paints were mixed) out of stone and they made ornaments out of sea shells. All of these crafts were also practiced by Mesoamerican cultures at this time.

The next period, known as the Colonial phase, saw the Hohokam territory expand. By this time, the Hohokam had become skilled farmers and their success allowed their culture to flourish. Canal systems became better developed and populations increased. New ideas, such as platform mounds and ball courts, became regular additions to Hohokam villages.

During the Colonial period, Hohokam pots became larger and painted designs were more common. Stone carvings were more

***Ball courts were long, open areas which were dug out of the soil. It is thought that ball courts were used as sites for ritual games or sports. Platform mounds were hard, flat areas used for ceremonial purposes.***

*This ball court site is in Wupatki National Monument, Arizona, homeland of the Sinagua people, but it is representative of a Hohokam ball court as well.*

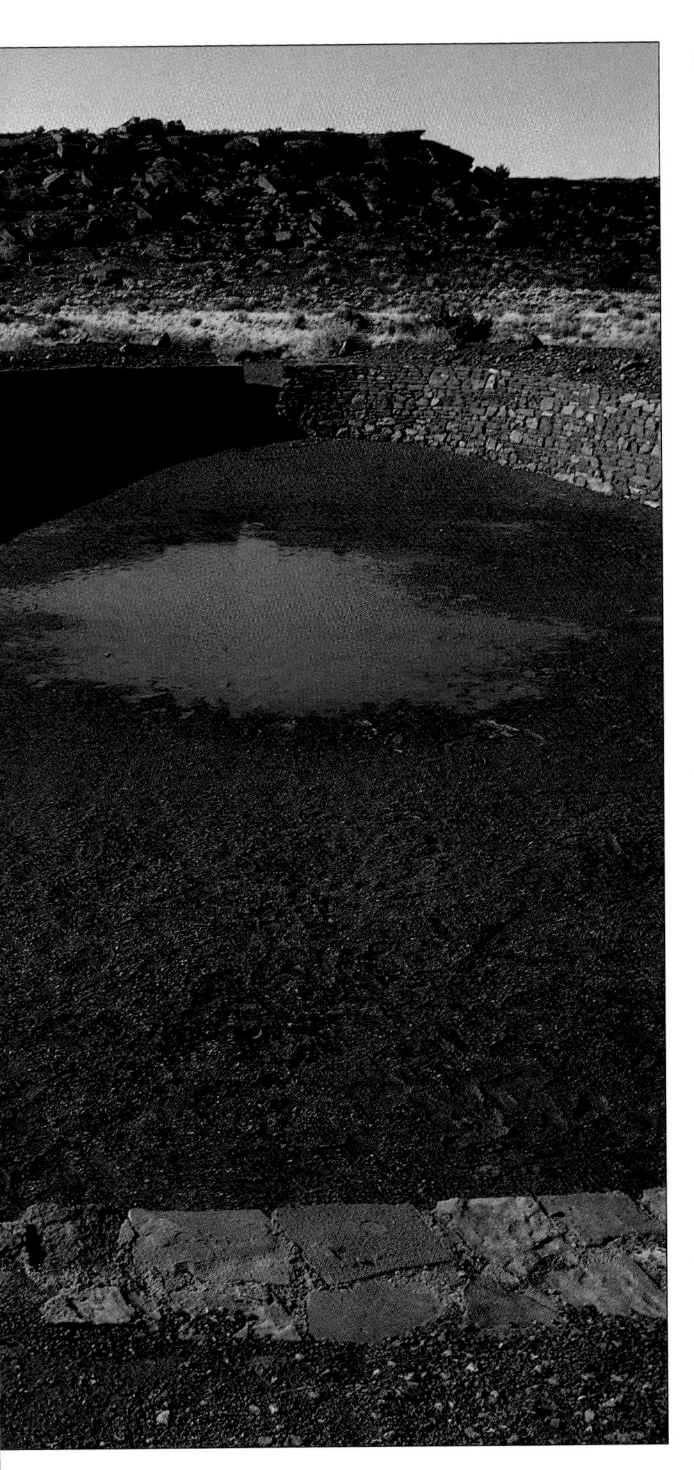

elaborate and simple mirrors made of reflective stones were introduced. Like the ball courts and platform mounds, these mirrors may have originated in Mesoamerica. The Colonial Hohokam, like their forebears, still built simple homes of brush and mud.

By 900 A.D., the Hohokam territory stopped expanding, and the Sedentary phase began. This was a time of little change. One exception was the introduction of shell etching. After creating a design on a sea shell with tree pitch, Hohokam artists then soaked the piece in fermented cactus juice. The acid in the juice ate away the shell, leaving behind an imprinted design. The Hohokam learned this technique several centuries before it was ever practiced in Europe. In fact, their etchings are thought to be the oldest in the world.

The Hohokam entered their final stage around 1100 A.D.. Known as the Classical

**QUESTION**

**What kinds of games do you play? If you were an archaeologist living 1,000 years from now, do you think you'd be able to guess the rules or meanings of today's games from the artifacts left behind?**

## QUESTION

**If the White House in Washington D.C. were someday abandoned and later discovered by archaeologists, do you think scientists would know that it was the home for all of the presidents of the United States? Maybe they would think it was a religious center, or a school, or a museum. What else might they think it was?**

phase, this era was marked by architectural changes as well as changes in lifestyle. By this time, the Hohokam domain was beginning to shrink, probably because of competition with other groups. They lived in fewer but larger sites. Hohokam farmers were beginning to till terraced hillsides, and towns were being built farther away from rivers. This meant even longer canals were needed.

Towards the end of the Classical period, the Hohokam built multi-storied structures known as Great Houses. The only remaining example is Casa Grande, 30 miles south of Phoenix, Arizona. Made out of adobe, this well-known Hohokam structure contains walls that are nearly five feet thick. It stood four stories high and required

*RIGHT: Detail of Casa Grande great house, Casa Grande Ruins National Monument, Arizona.*

*NEXT PAGE: A steel awning protects the crumbling structure of Casa Grande.*

*About 1450, the Hohokam returned to a simpler lifestyle that was no longer recognizable as Hohokam. There were probably many reasons why the Hohokam civilization faded: perhaps their irrigation systems failed, or the canals filled with soil, or the land became overused and infertile. Other causes, such as disease or raids by unfriendly neighbors, may have added to the fading of the Hohokam.*

200 tons of mud to build. The top story is a single large room, while lower levels consist of smaller chambers. The Park Service has now built a protective steel awning over the crumbling structure to protect it from the elements.

What purpose great houses served is still unclear. Some speculate that they were the homes of priests or chiefs, while others believe they were astrological observatories. Holes in the walls at Casa Grande align with the sun at key times of the year, such as the solstice. It may be that they were designed with defense in mind. Because the entire first story of Casa Grande is solid mud with no windows or doors, it must be entered by ladder. And surrounding the building and its village is a protective compound wall. The wall may also have been used to protect the area from animals and run-off rain water.

This new need for protection shows that the Hohokam may have been raided by unfriendly neighboring people. Their eventual collapse, however, was probably their own doing. Just as modern farmers have learned, years of intensive irrigation will raise the salinity, or salt content, of the soil, making it impossible for crops to grow. It is likely that the Hohokam suffered this calamity. Also, as with other prehistoric cultures in the Southwest, the Hohokam were plagued by years of drought. For these reasons, and perhaps others that remain a mystery, the Hohokam culture began to fade. By 1450 A.D., these once great canal builders had either moved away completely or they had reverted to a much simpler existence that was no longer recognizable as Hohokam.

*Hohokom petroglyph at Saguaro National Monument near Tucson, Arizona.*

# THE MOGOLLON

Thought to have descended from an Archaic group called the Cochise, the Mogollon were the first Southwesterners to adopt agriculture and other ideas from Mesoamerica. By 2000 B.C., their Archaic ancestors were growing corn and as early as 500 B.C., they were building permanent homes. Pottery was also introduced early into the Mogollon culture.

*Gila Cliff dwelling at Gila Cliff Dwellings National Monument, New Mexico.*

Living among the Mogollon Mountains of southwestern New Mexico and southeastern Arizona, the Mogollon people enjoyed an environment rich in natural resources. Unlike the desert lands of the Hohokam and the Anasazi, their mountainous territory included forests and grassy meadows. Game was plentiful here and streams offered reliable sources of water. Because the land provided many natural foods, the Mogollon people were under little pressure to grow their own. While the Mogollon did a little bit of farming, hunting and gathering still provided much of the food they needed to survive.

As with the Anasazi and Hohokam, archaeologists are still unsure when the Mogollon first appeared, however, 300 B.C. is a generally accepted date. While the core of their homeland

*The Gila River in the Mogollon homeland at Gila Cliff Dwellings, southwestern New Mexico.*

*Pit houses were permanent homes built partially underground, and entry was by way of ladder through a hole in the roof. Mogollon pit houses had entrances that faced east, perhaps to take advantage of the warm morning sunlight.*

was in the Mogollon Mountains, their world extended as far east as central New Mexico and south into Mesoamerica. The early Mogollon people lived in small villages built on hilltops, ridges and other places that could easily be defended. While the need for defense did not appear in the Anasazi and Hohokam cultures until much later, the Mogollon were faced with invasions during their earliest stages. It is thought that natural resources, such as food and water, may have been limited during this time and that because of this there may have been conflict between the Mogollon and some of their neighbors.

The first Mogollon dwellings were simple pit houses with entrances that faced east, perhaps to take advantage of the warming rays of the morning sun. Fire hearths were sometimes included and storage pits were either dug into the floor or in the ground nearby.

The Mogollon used the same pottery-making technique as the Anasazi. In fact, it is believed that the Mogollon passed the technology on to the Anasazi. Early Mogollon pots were usually plain, but some had a red slip. Because Mogollon pottery techniques resembled those of central Mexico, it is likely that they learned it from Mesoamerican craftsmen. The early Mogollon also made pipes out of clay, beaded bracelets, and pendants fashioned out of shells.

Around 500 A.D., the Mogollon people began to change back to a hunting and gathering lifestyle. They began eating more wild seeds, nuts, and roots, and relied less on crops they planted themselves. By 700 A.D., however, they once again began to grow their own food, thanks in part to the introduction of more nutritious strains of corn and improved farming techniques. At the same time, their populations began expanding as well.

The Mogollon experienced several major changes beginning

*Animals, mythical figures, and people performing everyday tasks are illustrated on Mimbres pottery created by the Mogollon.*

**QUESTION**

**Mogollon people ate wild seeds, nuts, roots and corn. They also ate rabbits, rodents and deer. What do you think was their favorite food? What is your favorite food? Do you think a Mogollon person your age would like to eat your favorite foods? Would you like to eat theirs?**

around 900 A.D.. For some unknown reason, they were now less concerned about defense, and so their settlements were built in the open, closer to their crops. Their villages were larger and, instead of living in pit houses, the Mogollon began building above-ground stone pueblos. The pit house tradition was continued in the construction of kivas, but unlike those of the Anasazi, Mogollon kivas were rectangular.

Mogollon pottery also underwent changes. Textured pottery began to appear around 300 A.D., but it was not until later that Mogollon pottery as we know it really began to appear. Among the new additions were bold black-on-white pots and bowls with highly distinctive designs. Named after the river valley in which it appeared, Mimbres Classic pottery featured fanciful depictions of animals, mythical figures, and people performing everyday tasks. So unusual

*Gila Cliff Dwellings, a Mogollon cliff dwelling in New Mexico.*

were these Mimbres wares that archaeologists have given the Mogollon special status as prehistoric artisans. Mogollon rock art during this time similarly featured beautiful depictions of animals and deities.

By 1000 A.D., enough changes had occurred to mark the start of the late Mogollon period. Although the Mogollon had greatly influenced the early Anasazi, by this time the roles had been reversed. Many characteristics of the Anasazi were accepted by the Mogollon, but the most striking influence is found in the architecture of the late period. In addition to building aboveground pueblos like the Anasazi, the Mogollon also began constructing cliff dwellings. Built after 1250 A.D., those found at Gila Cliff Dwellings National Monument are as elaborate as many that were built by the Anasazi.

Despite the influence of the Anasazi, the Mogollon eventually began showing signs of collapse and by 1300 A.D., they had almost completely abandoned the region. Why the Mogollon people left is still unclear, though again, drought is the leading theory. Their unique civilization, like that of other prehistoric people of the Southwest, was effectively lost in the centuries that followed.

# Other Peoples Of The Prehistoric Southwest

***In addition to the Anasazi, Hohokam and Mogollon, there were other cultures that flourished in the prehistoric Southwest. Some, such as the Sinagua and Salado, inhabited areas that lay between between the larger cultures. Often, these groups borrowed traits and ideas from their neighbors. Others, like the Fremont, lived on the fringes of the Southwest.***

**The Sinagua (Sa-nah-wah)**—By 600 A.D., small bands of Sinaguan farmers were living in an area which is now Flagstaff, Arizona. Sinagua is Spanish for "without water." The first Sinagua people lived in rounded pit houses, often at the edges of open meadows where farming was possible. The poor soil allowed for few crops, which in turn meant that early populations were never very big. For 400 years, life for the Sinagua changed little. But in 1064 A.D., the eruption of Sunset Crater in the San Francisco Peaks spewed lava, cinder and ash across the area. Once the earth quieted, the Sinagua found that the dark ash which covered the ground held moisture and captured the warmth of the sun. These conditions were excellent for farming and helped to bring about a flowering of the Sinagua culture.

As other peoples moved into the Sinagua homelands, a rich exchange of ideas took place. The Sinagua learned pueblo architecture from the Anasazi, ideas of irrigation and ball courts from the Hohokam, and a variety of pottery techniques from the Anasazi, Hohokam and Mogollon.

Drought and erosion probably caused the Sinagua to eventually abandon their homes between 1225 A.D. and 1400 A.D..

**The Salado (Sa-lah-doe)**—Although the origins of the Salado people are still uncertain, it is known that their homeland bordered that of the Anasazi, Hohokam and Mogollon. Because of this contact, the Salado culture included many traits which are also found in their neighbors.

In their desert valley, the Salado irrigated fields of corn, squash and beans with water from the Salt River. They built multi-roomed pueblos of cobblestone near their fields. They wove fine cotton fabric, and they created pottery with distinctive black-and-white-on-red designs.

For reasons still unknown, the Salado moved their home several times. Around 1300 A.D., they moved into the hills. Later they left the Tonto Basin completely and joined the Hohokam. The Salado and Hohokam shared many ideas, and it is thought that the Hohokam great houses, including Casa Grande, resulted from Salado influence. Salado multi-colored pottery also became popular with the Hohokam. Mounting environmental pressures, like drought and a depleted wood supply, probably forced the Salado to leave the area.

**The Fremont (Free-mont)**—Archaeologists believe that the Fremont originated from Archaic groups as early as 500 A.D.. They grew corn, but relied more on hunting and gathering than the Anasazi, and lived mostly in small settlements in pit houses. Interestingly, the Fremont sometimes lived in tipis and made shields, both of which are traits of Plains Indians rather than southwest cultures. The Fremont were unmatched in their elaborateness of their rock drawings, and today, impressive galleries of their art haunt hundreds of sites throughout the region.

Like other groups, the Fremont disappeared soon after A.D. 1300. Some archaeologists suggest that they became the Shoshoni or Paiute, while others believe they joined the Anasazi and drifted south.

*Sinugua ruins at Wupatki National Monument, Arizona*

# AFTERWORD

Despite all of the things that archaeologists have learned from the prehistoric ruins of the Southwest, there is still a lot that we don't know. Certainly, the countless artifacts that have been excavated show us how the inhabitants of the region survived, how they made their pottery and other tools, and when they lived. But what we do not know is why they did many of the things that they did. What were their religious beliefs? What did their rock art mean? And what made them leave their homelands?

*A ranger looks over damage from pot hunters in southwestern Colorado.*

To find the answers to these and other important questions, archaeologists will continue to sift through the ruins. And they will undoubtedly learn new methods or techniques that will help them better understand what they find. Because the future holds the promise of increased understanding of the prehistoric cultures of the region, it is important to protect all of the ruins found in the Southwest. While these sites may have survived for hundreds or even thousands of years, they are now being threatened by people who illegally dig up artifacts for profit. Called pot hunters, these thieves of time have disturbed thousands of prehistoric sites making it difficult for archaeologists to study them.

You can help stop this vandalism by following a few simple rules. When visiting a ruin, look but do not touch. This means leaving all pieces of pottery and other artifacts alone. Avoid climbing on dwelling walls because they are fragile, and do not touch, scratch, or draw on the petroglyphs and pictographs. Like the water we drink and the air we breathe, prehistoric ruins and artifacts are fragile resources that need to be protected so future generations can enjoy and learn from them, too.

*Prehistoric ruins and artifacts are fragile resources that need to be protected so that future generations can enjoy and learn from them. Many ancient artifacts are carelessly taken from their earthen homes by people who illegally dig them up for profit. In 1906, the Federal Antiquities Act was passed, making it illegal to remove ancient artifacts from a site.*

*Vandals have shot at this petroglyph in Northern New Mexico.*

# Glossary

**abandon**: to leave without meaning to return.
**adapt**: to change.
**adobe**: a brick made of sun-dried earth and straw.
**ancestor:** someone from whom a person is descended. Forefather, or forebear.
**archaic**: ancient; surviving from an earlier period.
**archaeology**: the study of what ancient people left behind, to understand the ancient people, their customs, and way of life.
**artifact**: an object made or used by humans representing a particular culture.
**artisan**: a skilled worker.
**atlatl**: (at-lat-el) throwing sticks used by prehistoric peoples to hunt.
**behavior**: the way a person or group responds to its environment.
**canal:** a channel or artificial waterway.
**canyon**: a deep, narrow valley with steep sides.
**ceramic**: made from clay and fired at a high temperature.
**ceremony**: a formal, ritual act.
**civilization**: the culture characteristic of a specific time or place.
**cliff dwelling:** an ancient, multi-storied, terraced structure built to house many people.
**cradle board:** a support used to carry an infant on the back.
**cremate:** to burn and reduce to ashes.
**crop:** a plant that can be grown and harvested for eating.
**culture:** the beliefs, social ways and material styles of a group of people.
**dendrochronology:** the science of dating events and weather patterns in former times by studying growth rings in trees.
**deplete:** to empty or to lessen.

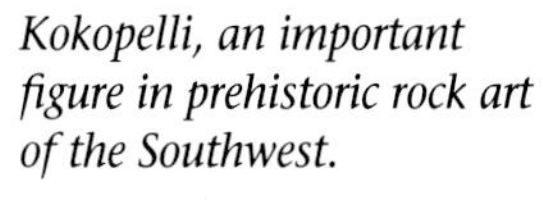

*Kokopelli, an important figure in prehistoric rock art of the Southwest.*

**descendant**: one coming from someone who lived before.
**dig**: a site where archaeologists search for artifacts.
**dwelling:** a shelter in which people live, as a house or building.
**excavate:** to dig out.
**extinct:** no longer in existence or living.
**forage:** to wander in search of food.
**Four Corners:** an area which crosses the borders of the states of New Mexico, Arizona, Colorado, and Utah.
**game:** wild animals hunted for food or sport.
**great houses**: multi-storied, adobe structures built by ancient people.
**growth ring:** an annual ring of growth that is seen in trees. Thick, light rings indicate a year of ample moisture; thin, dark rings indicate dry years.
**hunter-gatherer:** a method of survival in which people constantly move to find food—animals to hunt, and plants, seeds, and nuts to gather.
**hypothesis:** an assumption made to test its own logic and validity.
**irrigate:** to supply with water.
**kiva:** an underground room used by prehistoric and modern peoples for religious ceremonies.
**mano:** a stone used for milling and grinding.
**masonry:** something constructed of stone or brickwork.
**mesa:** a natural, flat-topped, elevated area.
**Mesoamerica:** Mexico.
**metate:** a stone grinding basin.
**midden:** a mound.
**migrate:** to move from one place or climate to another.
**monument:** a lasting reminder of something great.
**natural resource:** a material which is supplied by nature and can be used by humans, like mineral deposits, water and wood.
**nomadic:** moving about from place to place.
**overpopulation:** a condition of having too dense a population, causing damage to the environment and quality of life.
**petroglyph:** an ancient carving on a rock.
**pictograph:** an ancient drawing or painting on a rock wall.
**pit house:** a partially underground, permanent home built by ancient peoples, with a main living area and a smaller side area.
**pot hunter:** a person who illegally looks for and digs up ancient pots and other artifacts for profit.
**population:** the number of people, animals or plants in a region.
**pottery:** clayware, or earthenware.
**prehistoric:** belonging to a period before written history.
**pueblo:** a city or a village.
**radiocarbon dating:** a technique for dating objects that once lived by measuring amounts of radioactive carbon present in the objects.
**ruin(s):** the remains of something destroyed.
**site:** a location.
**slip:** the background color on painted pots.
**spear point:** the sharp tip which is attached to a shaft or spear.
**stratification:** layering of materials, as in artifacts layered in earth.
**teosinte:** a grass that is closely related to maize, or corn.
**trait:** a distinguishing quality.
**waddle-and-daub construction:** a method of building structures with packed mud and sticks.

# National Parks and Monuments

*To see prehistoric ruins and rock art today, visit the following sites:*

**ANASAZI**: Mesa Verde National Park, Chaco Culture National Historical Park, Aztec Ruins National Monument, Hovenweep National Monument, Canyonlands National Park, Natural Bridges National Monument, Canyon de Chelly National Monument, Navajo National Monument, Grand Canyon National Park, Petrified Forest National Park, El Morro National Monument, Bandelier National Monument, Petroglyphs National Monument, Pecos National Monument, and Salinas National Monument.

**HOHOKAM**: Casa Grande Ruins National Monument and Saguaro National Monument.

**MOGOLLON**: Gila Cliff Dwellings National Monument, the Gran Quivira unit of Salinas National Monument, and Three Rivers Petroglyph Site.

*Spruce Tree House, an Anasazi cliff dwelling in Mesa Verde National Park, Colorado.*

**SINAGUA:** Wupatki National Monument, Walnut Canyon National Monument, Montezuma Castle and Montezuma Well National Monuments, and Tuzigoot National Monument.

**SALADO:** Tonto National Monument.

**FREMONT**: Canyonlands National Park, Arches National Park, Dinosaur National Monument, and Colorado National Monument.

*Please refer to the map for locations of these national parks and monuments.*

# INDEX